Picking Apples

For Michael Smith
—M. M.

ALADDIN
An imprint of Simon & Schuster Children's Publishing Division
1230 Avenue of the Americas, New York, NY 10020
First Aladdin paperback edition September 2009
Text copyright © 2009 by Margaret McNamara
Illustrations copyright © 2009 by Mike Gordon
All rights reserved, including the right of reproduction in whole or in part in any form.
ALADDIN is a trademark of Simon & Schuster, Inc., and
related logo is a registered trademark of Simon & Schuster, Inc.
READY-TO-READ is a registered trademark of Simon & Schuster, Inc.
For information about special discounts for bulk purchases, please contact
Simon & Schuster Special Sales at 1-866-506-1949 or business@simonandschuster.com.
The Simon & Schuster Speakers Bureau can bring authors to your live event.
For more information or to book an event contact the Simon & Schuster Speakers
Bureau at 1-866-248-3049 or visit our website at www.simonspeakers.com.
Designed by Christopher Grassi
The text of this book was set in Century Schoolbook BT.
Manufactured in the United States of America
2   4   6   8   10   9   7   5   3
Library of Congress Cataloging-in-Publication Data
McNamara, Margaret.
Picking apples / by Margaret McNamara ;
illustrated by Mike Gordon. — 1st Aladdin ed.
p. cm. — (Ready-to-read) (Robin Hill School)
Summary: Michael refuses to help his classmates pick apples during a field trip until his
teacher, Mrs. Connor, finds the apple that is just right for him.
ISBN: 978-1-4169-5539-9 (pbk. edition)
0610 LAK
[1. Apples—Fiction. 2. School field trips—Fiction.] I. Gordon, Mike, 1948 Mar. 16– ill.
II. Title.
PZ7.M47879343Pic 2009
[E]—dc22
2009008056

Picking Apples

Written by Margaret McNamara
Illustrated by Mike Gordon

Ready-to-Read
Aladdin
New York London Toronto Sydney

Mrs. Connor's class
went on a field trip.

"Time for some
apple picking,"
Mrs. Connor said.

"I will not pick apples,"
said Michael.

Eigen climbed up
a pointy ladder.

He pulled down
twelve red apples.
"One dozen!" he said.

Ayanna and Hannah
picked apples
off the ground.

They found ten green apples.
"My back hurts!"
said Hannah.

Eigen and Becky
shook a tree.

Four red-and-green
apples fell down.
"That was easy," said Eigen.

Nick and Emma jumped up
and picked seven
speckled apples each.

"Hard work!" said Nick.

Katie sat on the ground
and waited till apples
fell into her lap.

She got two golden
apples that way.
"No sweat," said Katie.

The apples were
piling up.

Michael added zero
apples to the pile.

"Did you know apples
have names?"
asked Mrs. Connor.

"That is an Idared,"
said Mrs. Connor.

"Yum!" said Eigen.

"This one is a Honeycrisp,

and this
one is a
Russet,

and that one is a Crispin,"
said Mrs. Connor.

"Crisp!" said Ayanna.

"Boring," said Michael.

"And this one is for you,
Michael,"
said Mrs. Connor.

"What?" said Michael.

"It is a Granny Smith,"
  said Mrs. Connor.

"Smith?" said Michael.
"That is my name!
My name is Michael Smith."

"Now will you pick
some apples?"
asked Mrs. Connor.

"I pick this one!"
said Michael.
"The apple named for me!"